TRAINSTOP

BY BARBARA LEHMAN

HOUGHTON MIFFLIN COMPANY BOSTON

TO KATE

All rights reserved. For information about permission to
reproduce selections from this book, write to Permissions,
Houghton Mifflin Company, 215 Park Avenue South, New
York, New York 10003.

www.hmhbooks.com

The text of this book is set in Agenda.
The illustrations are watercolor, gouache, and ink.

Library of Congress Cataloging-in-Publication Data

Lehman, Barbara.
    Trainstop / by Barbara Lehman.
            p. cm.
    Summary: In this wordless picture book, a young girl
takes a train and makes a stop at a most unusual place
where she has an important task to perform.
    ISBN-13: 978-0-618-75640-7 (hc)
    ISBN-10: 0-618-75640-X (hc)
    [1. Railroads—Fiction. 2. Toys—Fiction. 3. Helpfulness—
Fiction. 4. Stories without words.] I. Title.

PZ7.L52176Tra2008
[E]—dc22
                                            2007061335

Printed in China
SCP 10 9 8 7 6 5 4 3
4500463088